Leprechauns Don't Play Fetch

Want more Bailey School Kids?

Check these out!

#1-46

SUPER SPECIALS #1-6

#1-10

And don't miss the...

HOLIDAY SPECIALS

Swamp Monsters Don't Chase Wild Turkeys

Aliens Don't Carve Jack-o'-lanterns

Mrs. Claus Doesn't Climb Telephone Poles

Leprechauns Don't Play Fetch

Coming soon . . .

Ogres Don't Hunt Easter Eggs

Leprechauns Don't Play Fetch

by Debbie Dadey
and
Marcia Thornton Jones

illustrated by John Steven Gurney

A
LITTLE APPLE
PAPERBACK

SCHOLASTIC INC.
New York Toronto London Auckland Sydney
Mexico City New Delhi Hong Kong Buenos Aires

To Barbara Beckham
and Randy Thornton
— MTJ

To the people at Scholastic
who gave us our start.
Many thanks!
— DD

ISBN 0-439-40833-4

12 11 10 7 8/0

Printed in the U.S.A. 40

First printing, February 2003

Contents

1

Fifty-Two Pickup

"No fair," Eddie griped. "It's the first warm day in March and we have to spend the entire weekend baby-sitting Aunt Mathilda's goofy dog in Sheldon City. We should be back home playing soccer."

"I think it's perfect," Howie told Eddie. "We get to stay with my grandmother while your aunt plays cards in the tournament. Then your aunt can drive my grandmother back to Bailey City for a St. Patrick's Day visit."

Eddie flopped down on the porch of Howie's grandmother's house. His friends, Howie, Melody, and Liza, sat in the grass. Eddie's aunt had just driven them all the way from Bailey City to Sheldon City.

"But what about me?" he asked. "What

am I supposed to do for fun this weekend?"

The words were barely out of Eddie's mouth when Diamond galloped across the yard and licked Eddie on the chin. Eddie pushed the giant dalmatian away. Then he tossed his blue ball cap for Diamond to fetch.

Liza dug deep into the pocket of her backpack and pulled out a deck of playing cards. "I think a card-playing tournament sounds exciting," she said.

Eddie grabbed the deck of cards from Liza's hands. "You want excitement?" he asked. "I'll teach you a very exciting game."

Liza grinned. "Now you're talking," she said.

"Gather 'round," Eddie told his friends. "Watch closely or you'll miss the fun." Eddie waited until his friends huddled around him. Diamond nosed between Liza and Howie.

"What's the name of your game?" Melody asked.

Eddie grinned and held the pack of cards high over his head. "It's called fifty-two pickup!"

With that, Eddie flung the deck in the air. Cards fluttered in the breeze and fell like rain all around the four friends. Diamond hopped up, trying to catch the cards in his mouth as they fell to the ground.

"No, Diamond!" Liza screamed. "Those are brand-new!"

Melody, Howie, and Liza dove to the ground, hurrying to gather up the cards before the big spotted dog could eat them. Just as Melody grabbed for the king of clubs, Diamond leaned over and licked Melody's face from her chin to her forehead.

"Yuck," Melody yelped, pushing Diamond away. "I'm covered in dog slobber! Doesn't this beast have any manners?"

"Of course he does," Eddie said. "I trained him myself."

"That explains it all," Liza said with a giggle. "Eddie is the biggest beast this side of the Mississippi River!"

Eddie was ready to flick a handful of cards right in Liza's face, but his aunt and Howie's grandmother came out on the porch before he had a chance.

"Look at the wee ones. They seem to be having the time of their lives." Howie's grandmother had just moved to Sheldon City from Ireland and she didn't know Eddie very well.

Eddie's aunt, on the other hand, knew all about Eddie. She pushed her ball cap down over her gray curls and glared at Eddie until he politely handed Liza her cards. "I think these kids need a little sweetening up," Eddie's Aunt Mathilda said. "They've been cooped up in the van with me all morning."

Eddie's eyes widened and Liza grinned as Aunt Mathilda reached into the pocket

of her jeans and pulled out a wad of money. "There's a candy store three blocks down the road," she told them. "This money is yours as long as you agree to take good care of Diamond while I'm at the tournament."

Eddie hopped up from the porch and flung his arm around the big dog's neck. "Diamond is my buddy," Eddie said. "You have nothing to worry about, Aunt Mathilda. Nothing at all."

2

Clover Patch Pet Store

Eddie and Diamond led Howie, Melody, and Liza down the sidewalk toward the candy store. As they waited at the light to cross the street, Liza pointed to a small shop that sat back from the road. "What kind of place is that?" she asked.

A small white store with bright green shutters stood behind at least seventeen tall trees and an overgrown yard of clover. A sign that matched the shutters spelled out CLOVER PATCH PET STORE.

"I bet they'd have a bone for Diamond," Eddie said.

At the sound of his name, Diamond darted up to the pet shop door. The kids had no choice but to follow.

"This will only take a few minutes," Eddie told his friends. "I promise."

A bell jingled as the four kids stepped into the small shop. The front room was filled with tanks of fish. A large white bird perched near the door shrieked as soon as they entered.

"Well, now," a friendly voice called from the back of the store. "It sounds like I might be having visitors."

A short man wearing a crooked hat and a leather apron over his green coveralls stepped out from the back room. Three leather pouches dangled from his belt and he spoke with an Irish brogue just like Howie's grandmother. The man smiled, but he stepped back into the shadows as soon as he saw Diamond.

"Hi, I'm Eddie. These are my friends and this is my dog, Diamond," Eddie said.

"My name is Mr. McDawgle," the storeowner answered as he stared at the dalmatian. "I see you'll be needing a big bone for a big beast. I have just the thing for you."

The man hurried behind the counter

and grabbed a rawhide bone from a bin. He was so short, his head barely showed above the counter. "This is just the thing your dog would be wanting," he said, holding up the bone.

At the sight of the bone, Diamond jumped up and put two giant paws on the counter. Mr. McDawgle leaped back, keeping far away from Diamond's drooling tongue. "Oh, my," he said, wiping sweat from his forehead. "Perhaps your dog would be happy to wait outside."

Mr. McDawgle reached into a pouch on his belt and pulled out a doggy treat. He tossed it across the room. Diamond caught sight of the treat and raced to catch it.

"Come on," Eddie said as he grabbed Diamond by the collar and pushed him outside. Diamond sat by the door and whined.

"Mr. McDawgle acts like he's afraid of Diamond," Melody whispered.

"Don't be silly," Howie said softly. "I'm

pretty sure a pet store owner wouldn't be afraid of dogs."

"Maybe he's just being safe," Liza said. "Mr. McDawgle doesn't know Diamond. It's always a good idea to stay away from strange dogs, especially big ones like Diamond."

As soon as Diamond was outside, Mr. McDawgle stepped out from behind the counter.

"That's better," Mr. McDawgle said. "Now, let me be showing you around the shop."

"Where are the puppies?" Liza asked.

The bounce left Mr. McDawgle's step and his forehead creased in a frown. "The Clover Patch has not the space for dogs of any shape or size," he said. "You'll not find a single one inside my shop, but I do rent kennel space behind the store to the Humane Society. They'd be the ones you should see about adopting a canine beast."

Liza took a step back, suddenly not

liking the way Mr. McDawgle sounded. "We'd better go to the candy store now," Liza whispered to her friends.

"In just a minute," Eddie said, "I want to see the snakes."

Mr. McDawgle's face turned red. "You'll not be finding a snake at the Clover Patch, either," he assured them. "Where I come from, we rid the land of snakes, we hated them so."

The kids couldn't take their eyes off Mr. McDawgle as he showed them around the store. Even Diamond stood at the door with his ears perked up, listening to the storeowner. "You sure do like animals," Melody finally said.

Mr. McDawgle blushed and looked down at his feet. "Animals are the sunshine of my life," he told her. "They remind me of a little verse I shared with my mum when I was but a wee lad." Mr. McDawgle closed his eyes and smiled before telling the rhyme.

My shop is a pet treasure chest.
And I'm not saying this in jest.
You should buy what I say
From my great pet display.
My supplies for your pets are the
best!

Smiling, Mr. McDawgle swept his hand toward all the supplies that crowded the Clover Patch Pet Store. "Now, what might you be wanting to buy today?"

Without thinking, Liza bought a collar for a dog she didn't have. Melody bought fish food, but she had no fish. Howie paid for a fuzzy mouse for a kitten he didn't own. Eddie bought a newt and a dog bone.

The kids were halfway back to Howie's grandmother's house when Liza stopped in the middle of the sidewalk. Eddie didn't notice and ran right into her. "What's the big idea?" Eddie snapped.

Liza looked at the dog collar dangling

from her hand. "Hey," she said. "What just happened?"

Melody peeked into the plastic box at Eddie's newt. "I'm not sure," she said, "but I think I know what's going to happen."

Eddie nodded, realizing they had spent all their candy money. "I think we're going to be in BIG trouble!"

3

Mrs. Jeepers

"Look," Melody said as she pointed toward a tall woman with bright red hair.

"Oh, no," Liza said with a gulp. "What's Mrs. Jeepers doing here?"

"Sheesh," Eddie complained. "Why would our teacher follow us all the way to Sheldon City?"

The kids shivered. Each of them suspected their teacher might be a blood-sucking vampire and that the mysterious green brooch she always wore had powerful magic that could make even Eddie behave. Diamond yipped and hid behind a tree as Mrs. Jeepers walked closer.

"Good afternoon, children," Mrs. Jeepers said in her Transylvanian accent. "What a pleasure to see you."

"Hello," Liza said politely. "We're visiting Howie's grandmother."

Mrs. Jeepers nodded. "I see you have bought interesting items."

Melody held up her fish food and Liza showed Mrs. Jeepers the dog collar. Howie blushed when he pulled his fuzzy mouse out of a bag.

"What did you buy?" Mrs. Jeepers asked Eddie.

Eddie held up his box so that Mrs. Jeepers could see his newt. "What a lovely creature," Mrs. Jeepers said. "But I did not know you wanted a newt."

Eddie shrugged. "Well, I didn't really want it."

"Then why did you buy it?" Mrs. Jeepers asked.

Eddie's face turned red. He opened his mouth, but he wasn't sure what to say.

CLOVER PATCH PET SHOP
CLOVER
PATCH
PET SHOP
FISH
FOOD

Why had he bought the newt? He really didn't know.

"Liza, I didn't know you had a dog," Mrs. Jeepers continued.

Liza put the dog collar behind her back. "Well, I don't have a dog," Liza said, "but this collar was so pretty. I just couldn't resist."

Melody nodded. "I don't have a fish, either, but for some reason I really wanted to buy fish food."

Howie looked down at the cat toy in his hand. "I don't have a cat," Howie admitted. "But when Mr. McDawgle, the pet store owner, started talking about this fuzzy mouse, I just had to have it."

"That's it!" Melody yelled. "Mr. McDawgle talked us into all this stuff."

Mrs. Jeepers smiled her odd little half smile. "It sounds like the store owner is full of blarney."

"What's blarney?" Liza asked.

"In Ireland, there is a legend," Mrs. Jeepers told them. "If anyone kisses the fabled Blarney stone, they will be able to talk anyone into anything."

"Yuck," Eddie said. "Kissing a rock is disgusting! I don't believe in kissing anybody or anything!"

"Maybe Mr. McDawgle did kiss the Blarney stone," Howie said with a grin. "After all, he is from Ireland."

The smile drained from Mrs. Jeepers' face. "What does this pet store owner look like?" she asked.

As soon as Liza described him, Mrs. Jeepers touched the green brooch at her throat. "I think I must visit this Mr. McDawgle myself."

The kids watched Mrs. Jeepers go into the Clover Patch Pet Store. "Do you think Mrs. Jeepers will get our money back for us?" Liza asked hopefully.

Howie shook his head. "More than likely Mr. McDawgle will talk her into buying a pet chicken for the classroom."

Liza and Melody giggled, but Eddie remained serious. "I just hope that Mr.

McDawgle doesn't let Mrs. Jeepers kiss the Blarney stone."

"Why is that?" Howie asked.

Eddie gulped. "Because if Mrs. Jeepers gets the gift of blarney, she'll be able to talk us into anything!"

4

Blarney

"No more money," Aunt Mathilda told Eddie. It was the next day and they were in Howie's grandmother's kitchen. "Too much candy will rot your teeth."

Eddie groaned. He didn't want to tell Aunt Mathilda he'd used his candy money to buy a newt and a dog bone instead of licorice and gum balls. Prince Diamond looked up from his bone with slobber dripping down his jowls.

"How about a lovely cup of tea?" Howie's grandmother suggested.

Eddie smiled. "Thank you. That would be very nice."

Eddie went out onto the front porch with his tea. He poured the drink onto a bush and sat on the steps with a sigh. His

friends were already sitting there. "This has to be the worst weekend ever," Eddie complained.

Liza shook her head. "Why did you take that tea if you weren't going to drink it?"

Eddie shrugged. "Maybe Howie's grandmother has the gift of blarney, too. She talked me into it."

"That Mr. McDawgle makes me so mad," Melody said. "We would have plenty of candy if it wasn't for him."

"We ought to go over to that pet store right now and ask him to give us our money back," Howie said.

Eddie jumped up from the step. "That's it!" he yelled. "I'll tell that little pet store owner that we know he tricked us and demand our money back."

"We can't do that," Liza said nervously. "We're just kids."

Melody stood up beside Eddie. "Kids have rights, too. Mr. McDawgle shouldn't have talked us into buying things we don't need. It wasn't fair."

"Fair, shmair," Eddie said, pounding his hand into his fist. "I'm ready for justice."

"Let's go," Howie said with a determined nod.

"Aunt Mathilda!" Eddie yelled. "We'll be right back."

Eddie snapped a leash onto Diamond's collar. The kids gathered up their receipts and pet supplies and ran down the street toward the pet shop.

"Don't you think we should bring an adult with us?" Liza asked.

Eddie puffed out his chest as he ran. "We don't need adults. We have me. Super Eddie!"

Melody laughed. "Faster than a speeding ant and able to leap over small buildings with the help of a helicopter. That's Eddie."

Eddie turned his head and stuck out

his tongue at Melody. Unfortunately, he didn't see the lamppost in front of him.

"Look out!" Liza cried, but it was too late.

Wham! Eddie slammed into the post and crumpled to the ground.

5

Blarney Magic

The bells over the door jingled a merry tune when Howie, Melody, Liza, and Eddie entered the Clover Patch Pet Store. Eddie rubbed the bump on his forehead before tripping over a lady and her fluffy white dog.

"Sorry," Eddie said. He backed up, knocking into a little girl who was looking at ferret toys. He hopped out of her way only to bump an old man searching for a parrot perch.

Liza grabbed Eddie's elbow and pulled him safely to the side. "Watch where you're going," she whispered.

"It's not my fault," Eddie grumbled. "Where did all these people come from?"

"The shop is much busier than yesterday," Howie agreed.

FERRET TOYS

The four friends looked around the pet store. Customers dug through the cat toys, browsed for doggie treats, and gawked at the lizards, hamsters, and fish. In fact, there were so many people in the store that Eddie had to push his way through the crowd to get near the cash register.

"The pet business must really be booming," Melody said as they found a place at the back of a long line.

The bells over the door jingled and jangled as people left and more people came in. The kids could hear Diamond whining outside every time the door opened.

"Maybe Mr. McDawgle placed an ad in the newspaper," Liza said.

"Or maybe Mrs. Jeepers was right," Melody said with a giggle. "Mr. McDawgle is full of blarney. He's talking everyone in Sheldon City into buying pet supplies that they don't need."

Howie nodded. "After all," he added,

"Mr. McDawgle is from Ireland and that's where Blarney Castle stands."

"It's also where leprechauns hide pots of gold," Liza said, laughing out loud. "So if Mr. McDawgle has blarney magic then maybe he's a leprechaun, too!"

"Mr. McDawgle doesn't need a pot for his money," Eddie said, pointing to the three leather pouches swaying from the storeowner's belt. Each pouch was lumpy and full. "He carries his treasure on his belt, and it's not gold. It's full of the money he talked out of poor unsuspecting customers like us!"

"That's not money in those pouches," Howie said. "The money is in the cash register. Mr. McDawgle probably has different kinds of treats in those bags for the animals in his store."

It seemed as if Howie was right because just then a lady with purple fingernails walked up to Mr. McDawgle. Her white mop of a dog tugged at its leash. As soon as Mr. McDawgle saw the dog, he fished into one of his pouches and threw a doggie treat far across the floor. The dog scrambled after it.

"A lovely pooch you have, my dear lady," Mr. McDawgle said. "And I know just what your poochie would be a-wanting."

Mr. McDawgle plucked a brush from a nearby display. "This will leave the lassie's hair silky and shiny."

The woman snatched the brush from Mr. McDawgle's hand. "You are absolutely right. My little Muffin will be so happy when I brush her with this," the lady said as she hurried to the end of the long line of people at the counter.

"Mr. McDawgle could talk the warts off a toad," Eddie huffed.

"Just like he talked you into buying a newt," Liza added.

"He can talk anyone into anything," Melody said. "Just listen to what he's telling that kid with the kitten!"

The four friends stopped talking so that they could hear Mr. McDawgle's lilting words. A chubby boy with a face full of freckles was cuddling a gray kitten.

"That kitten is the perfect pet for a lad such as yourself," Mr. McDawgle was saying.

The boy scratched the kitten's chin. "My parents think I'm too young for a pet," he said sadly.

"Nonsense," Mr. McDawgle said. "In fact, I have a little rhyme for you."

A cat is the pet meant for you,
Instead of bowwow, it goes mew.
You will like the soft fur
And the musical purr
Of this kitten named Hullabaloo!

"Hullabaloo!" the freckled boy shouted. "That's a perfect name for a perfect kitten. I'll take her!"

Liza gasped. "His mom or dad should be here! What if they don't want him to have a kitten?"

"What if Eddie's grandmother doesn't want him to have a newt?" Melody added.

Eddie's face turned bright pink. He knew his grandmother would have a fit if she found out about the newt. That was the real reason he was determined to get his money back, but he wasn't about to admit it. "My grandmother has nothing to do with it. I want my money back so I can go to the candy store," he told his friends. "I don't want this newt!" The newt scurried under a leaf at Eddie's words.

That's exactly what Eddie told Mr. McDawgle when it was their turn in line. Melody, Liza, and Howie put the collar, cat toy, and fish food beside the newt on the counter along with their receipts. "We don't want these, either," Liza said politely.

Mr. McDawgle tapped the top of the fish food with his finger. "Now I am a-thinking what you'll be needing is something more fitting to your sweet dispositions."

“That’s exactly what we need!” Eddie said with a grin. “Something sweet. Like candy!”

Mr. McDawgle didn’t reach into the cash register for money. Instead, he spoke one of his rhymes.

For Melody kitty-cat litter,
Since purring kittens would fit her.
We’ll get Liza a fish,
And for Howie a dish,
Then a muzzle for Eddie, yes sir!

6

Allergies?

The four friends slumped under the shade of one of the trees in front of the pet store. Diamond ran to each of them, his tail wagging. He tried to get someone to play with him, but Melody, Howie, Eddie, and Liza weren't interested. Diamond finally plopped to the ground with a grunt.

Melody sat on a bag of kitty litter. Liza held a tiny fish in a little round bowl. Howie stared at the dog dish in his lap. Eddie kicked at a muzzle with his sneakers.

"How did this happen?" Eddie moaned. "We went in there to get our money back and we ended up with more useless pet supplies."

"Everything was going fine until Mr.

McDawgle started spouting rhymes," Melody said.

Liza nodded. "I never thought I'd want a fish until he mentioned it."

"I sure don't need a dog's water bowl," Howie said. "But I guess I can use it for one of my science experiments."

"Well, the last thing I need is a muzzle," Eddie griped.

Howie smiled. Liza giggled. Melody laughed out loud. "Actually," Melody said, "a muzzle is the perfect thing for you."

"Very funny," Eddie said with a sneer. He curled his fingers around the muzzle and tossed it as far as he could.

Diamond jumped up and darted after it. "That dog would play fetch with a porcupine," Eddie grumbled.

It was true. Diamond carried the muzzle back to Eddie and waited for him to throw it again.

Eddie threw the muzzle, but he wasn't happy about it. In fact, nobody was smiling. Diamond was the only happy one in

Kitty-Poo

the bunch. As long as Eddie threw the muzzle, Diamond raced across the yard and brought it back. If Eddie didn't throw it, Diamond would drop it at Melody, Liza, or Howie's feet.

"Enough already," Melody said. "We have more important things to do than play fetch."

"Like what?" Liza asked.

"We still have to get our money back," Melody told her.

"Melody is right," Eddie blurted. "Mr. McDawgle sold us things we don't need. It's all his fault."

"Wait a second," Howie said calmly. "It's not his fault we decided to buy these things. He just suggested them. We could have said no."

"Howie is right," Liza said. "It's my own fault that I'm stuck with a fish instead of a bag full of chocolate."

Eddie flopped back in the grass and sighed. "There is no way I'm keeping a worthless muzzle," he said as Diamond dropped the muzzle beside Eddie's feet again. Eddie was tired of throwing. He was tired of the muzzle. He covered his eyes with his arm and ignored Diamond.

Just then, the door to Clover Patch Pet Store swung open. Mr. McDawgle hurried outside. He wore boots, bright green coveralls, and green leather gloves. Five dogs on leashes pulled him across the lawn.

"Those must be the dogs the Humane Society has up for adoption," Melody said.

"Why in the world is Mr. McDawgle wearing gloves to walk them?" Howie asked. "It's not cold outside."

"Maybe he's allergic to dogs," Liza said.

"That would make sense," Howie said. "Remember how he avoided Diamond?"

"And he didn't get near that little white dog," Melody said.

"I'm sure Mr. McDawgle will be fine as

long as he doesn't actually touch a dog," Liza said.

Unfortunately, Diamond's ears perked up as soon as he saw the other dogs. His tail started wagging. Then, before the kids could say, "The luck of the Irish be with you," Diamond took off running.

7

Leprechaun

"Come back here," Eddie yelled as he chased after Diamond. Liza, Melody, and Howie raced after the dog, too. It was like a St. Patrick's Day parade with five dogs leading a short man wearing green, a galloping spotted dog, and four frantic kids down the sidewalk. Diamond didn't stop running until he reached the park.

The kids were panting by the time they finally caught up with Diamond. "Isn't that sweet?" Liza said. "Mr. McDawgle is playing fetch with the dogs."

"And talking to them," Howie added. The kids watched as the pet store owner threw sticks. Diamond joined right in. Every time a dog brought back a stick, Mr. McDawgle praised the dog and gave it a treat — as long as the dog dropped

the stick in the grass. "Good boy," he said. "But don't be getting too close."

"I don't care if he's doing the hokey-pokey," Eddie snapped. "I want my money back, and I'm going to get it right now."

Liza grabbed Eddie's arm. "Wait," she said. "There's something weird about Mr. McDawgle. I didn't notice it before."

Howie nodded. "I think so, too, but I can't figure out what it is."

"He could charm the skin off a snake," Melody admitted.

"Not a snake," Howie said. "Remember, Mr. McDawgle hates snakes."

"He is from Ireland," Liza said. "I don't think they have snakes there."

"That's because St. Patrick drove the snakes from Ireland hundreds of years ago," Howie said.

"That's a legend," Melody told them as she stooped down to pick a four-leaf clover. "Just like the leprechauns."

"That's it!" Howie yelled. "Mr. McDawgle is a leprechaun!"

KITTY

Proof

"Your mind has turned to clover," Eddie told Howie.

"Leprechauns don't sell guppies," Liza agreed. "They don't own pet stores. And they don't live in Sheldon City."

"Leprechauns definitely don't play fetch," Melody said, nodding toward Mr. McDawgle.

"I have proof," Howie said as he held up his thumb. "First of all, he wears green."

Eddie snickered. "I'm wearing a red shirt. I guess that makes me Santa Claus. Ho, ho, ho!"

"If that's true, you have to give me all your toys," Melody said.

"Very funny," Howie said, raising a finger. "But that's not all. His shop is right beside a clover patch."

"My dad uses weed killer to get rid of clover in our yard," Melody said. "Maybe Mr. McDawgle doesn't know about weed killer."

"It's also down the street from the beach, but that doesn't make Mr. McDawgle a sea monster," Liza pointed out.

"But he does know about limericks," Howie continued and held up another finger.

"What's a limerick?" Eddie asked as his stomach rumbled. "Is that a new type of candy?"

Liza giggled. "A limerick is a silly poem. The rhymes almost put you in a trance."

"They're used by leprechauns," Howie said, holding up the rest of the fingers on one hand. "And Mr. McDawgle wears a hat and those funny leather pouches. He won't look anyone in the eyes."

Melody clapped her hands. "That's because you can gain control over a leprechaun by looking in their eyes. Howie's grandmother told us that."

"Exactly. And leprechauns are known tricksters. Mr. McDawgle is a leprechaun and he's tricking all the people of Sheldon City out of their money to add to his own pot of gold," Howie said.

"But leprechauns are supposed to be shy," Melody told Howie. "Mr. McDawgle loves talking to people."

"He talks up a storm," Eddie added. "He's so full of blarney he can talk the spots off Diamond's back."

"No, he couldn't," Liza pointed out. "Mr. McDawgle won't get close to Diamond."

Howie's face turned pale. "This is worse than I thought," he said. "Not only is Mr. McDawgle a leprechaun, but he's kissed the Blarney stone!"

9

Leprechaun Worries

"So what if he's kissed the Blarney stone?" Eddie wanted to know. "As long as I get my money back for this muzzle, I never have to see him again."

"We can't let a sweet-talking leprechaun loose in Sheldon City," Howie argued.

"Why should I care?" Eddie asked. "When Aunt Mathilda drives us back to Bailey City, we'll leave these leprechaun worries behind."

Liza shook her head. "Howie is right. We have to do something. Mr. McDawgle is convincing people to buy pets they never thought they wanted."

"But that's a good thing," Melody pointed out. "There are lots of homeless pets. Mr. McDawgle is finding them homes."

"Not really. Think of that boy who adopted a kitten," Liza reminded her friend. "He didn't have his parents' permission and he might not be able to take care of it. What if his parents make him get rid of it?"

"It wouldn't be fair to the kitten," Eddie said.

"Buying a pet is a big responsibility," Liza said. "We have to save those poor animals from getting stuck in homes where they're not wanted."

"That's what I've been saying!" Howie shouted.

"Duck," Melody squealed. The kids quickly hid behind a tree as Mrs. Jeepers strode across the park, straight toward Mr. McDawgle.

"What is she doing here?" Melody whispered.

Eddie sighed. "I don't know, but it's

never a good thing when a teacher shows up. Especially when that teacher is Mrs. Jeepers!"

"She looks mad," Liza said with a whimper.

Liza was right. Mrs. Jeepers stopped in front of Mr. McDawgle. The pet store owner was so short Mrs. Jeepers towered over him. The five dogs hunkered down. Diamond took one look at Mrs. Jeepers and tucked his tail firmly between his legs.

"I wish I could hear what she's saying," Howie said.

"Maybe we could sneak closer," Eddie said. He was an expert at sneaking. If anyone could spy on Mrs. Jeepers, it would be Eddie. This time he didn't have a chance.

"Wait," Melody warned. "Something is happening."

Mr. McDawgle reached into one of his pouches. He pulled out a small item and held it up so Mrs. Jeepers could see it.

"What is it?" Liza asked.

Melody squinted so she could get a better look. "It looks like a pebble or a little piece of a rock," Melody told her.

Mrs. Jeepers gently rubbed her brooch as she admired the item.

Howie gasped. "What if it's a chip from the Blarney stone," he asked, "and Mrs. Jeepers kisses it? She'll have the gift of gab. She'll be able to talk us into doing anything she wants."

"Kissing anything sounds disgusting, if you ask me," Eddie said with a snicker. But his laugh was cut short when Mrs. Jeepers suddenly bent over and kissed the tiny pebble in Mr. McDawgle's hand.

10

Too Late

Eddie slapped his forehead and groaned. "She did it! She kissed the Blarney stone!"

"We're in BIG trouble now!" Howie yelled.

"Shhh," Melody warned.

The kids held their breaths. Liza crossed her fingers. The four kids stared at Mrs. Jeepers and Mr. McDawgle, hoping they hadn't heard Howie.

They had. Both adults turned and glared at the four kids huddled behind the tree. The kids froze in fear, but Diamond ran up to Mr. McDawgle and snatched the stone out of his gloved hand.

"Get that dog!" Mr. McDawgle cried. Mrs. Jeepers grabbed at Diamond, but the dog darted away.

"Let's get out of here!" Liza squealed.

"We can't leave without Diamond," Eddie told her.

Howie whistled. Liza clapped her hands. Melody shouted. "Here, Diamond!"

Diamond's ears perked up and he looked their way, but the spotted dog didn't budge. He stared at Mr. McDawgle's pouch, hoping for another treat.

Mrs. Jeepers and Mr. McDawgle took a step in the kids' direction. Liza's face turned as white as clover blossoms. "What are we going to do?" Liza whimpered.

"Never fear," Eddie said, "Super Eddie is here."

Before Mrs. Jeepers and Mr. McDawgle could take another step, Eddie grabbed the muzzle he'd bought and shook it over his head. Diamond sat up, staring at the dangling leather in Eddie's hand. "FETCH!" Eddie yelled. Then he threw the muzzle as hard as he could toward the sidewalk.

Diamond sprinted into action. He jumped over two dogs and dashed between a third and fourth. There was nothing the kids could do to stop him. Diamond darted between Mr. McDawgle and Mrs. Jeepers, knocking them both flat to the ground.

"RUN!" Eddie screamed. "Run for your lives."

That's just what the kids did. Diamond grabbed the muzzle and chased the running kids. They didn't stop until they reached Howie's grandmother's house. They galloped up the steps, pushed Diamond inside, and then snapped the lock tight.

"Do you think Mrs. Jeepers will find us here?" Liza asked.

Howie shook his head. "She doesn't know where my grandmother lives," he said, but he didn't sound very sure.

"A vampire teacher could find out something like that," Eddie argued. He parted the curtains covering the living

room window and looked outside. "Oh, no!" he gasped.

Melody, Liza, and Howie scrambled over the couch to peek out the window. Mrs. Jeepers and Mr. McDawgle were walking down the sidewalk, straight toward Howie's grandmother's house.

The kids fell back on the couch. "Let's sneak out the back door," Melody suggested.

Howie shook his head. "She'd see us leaving. Maybe we should call the police."

"What would we tell them?" Eddie asked. "That a leprechaun and a vampire teacher are chasing us?"

Liza's lips trembled. "They'd never believe us."

"We have to think of something," Melody said, "before it's too late."

Just then, the doorknob to the front door turned. "I think," Eddie whispered, "it's already too late!"

11

Kiss

The kids stared in horror as the door slowly swung open. Liza gulped when a gnarled hand reached through the opening. One wrinkled face and then another smiled at the kids.

"It's Aunt Mathilda," Eddie said in relief.

"And Grandma," Howie said, hugging his grandmother around the waist.

Eddie's Aunt Mathilda laughed. "Who were you expecting? Spider-Man?"

Eddie shook his head, but Howie didn't waste any time. "Grandma," he asked. "What can you tell us about the Blarney stone?"

Howie's grandmother chuckled and took a seat on the flowered couch. "What would you be wanting to know?"

"Well," Melody explained. "We know that if you kiss the Blarney stone it gives you the gift of blarney."

"But what we really need to know is . . ." Liza began.

"Is there any way to get rid of the blarney?" Eddie finished the question for Liza.

Aunt Mathilda handed Howie's grandmother a cup of tea. Howie's grandmother took a sip before answering. "Saints preserve us. There is only one way, but why would nice young children like you be needing to know?"

Liza looked at her sneakers. Eddie picked at a scab on his elbow. Melody drummed her fingers on the table. The kids knew she would never believe the truth. Finally, Howie grinned. "For research," he fibbed. "We need to know for a school report!"

"Well, then," Howie's grandmother said with a smile. "I suppose I can be telling you for your research. 'Tis known by just

a few. The only cure against the magic of the Blarney stone is a kiss. The kiss of a beast!"

"A kiss!" Eddie blurted. "A kiss is the cure?"

Howie's grandmother laughed until tears spotted her cheeks. "Aye," she said with a nod. "And only a kiss will do!"

Once the kids were settled on the porch and were sure Eddie's aunt and Howie's grandmother couldn't hear them, Eddie flopped back and sighed. He still had peanut butter on his face from lunch. "The kiss of a beast!" he groaned. "Where will we find a beast?"

Just then, Diamond jumped up on Eddie's chest and licked the peanut butter off his cheek.

"Diamond!" Liza squealed. "Diamond's the answer!"

"What are you talking about?" Eddie asked.

"Diamond is a beast," Liza explained. "All dogs are beasts!"

"And dogs are the only beasts in a pet shop that kiss," Melody added with a giggle when Diamond licked her right across the cheek. "That's why Mr. McDawgle won't get close to dogs. They're kissing beasts!"

Howie nodded. "I think I get it now. If Diamond kisses Mr. McDawgle, then our problems will be over."

"Are you sure it will work?" Eddie asked.

"We have to try," Melody said. "The future of Sheldon City depends on us."

"And on Diamond," Liza said.

Eddie looked at his friends. Then he looked at Diamond. Diamond wagged his tail. "Okay," he said. "Let's do it!"

Eddie snapped the leash to Diamond's collar, then the four friends raced to the crowded pet shop. Mr. McDawgle was busy helping a lady with gray hair pick out an iguana. He was right in the middle of reciting a limerick when Eddie interrupted him.

"Hello, Mr. McDawgle," Eddie said loud enough for everyone in the store to hear. "We have a present for you."

Mr. McDawgle grinned, but the smile faded from his face when he spied Diamond. "Just what would this surprise be?"

Eddie gently shoved Diamond toward Mr. McDawgle. "Go ahead, Diamond, give him the surprise."

Mr. McDawgle was too quick. He pulled a treat from a pouch and tossed it out the door as a new customer entered. Diamond galloped out of the store and tackled the treat without another glance at Mr. McDawgle.

"So much for that great plan," Eddie said. "Now what do we do?"

The kids watched as Mr. McDawgle frowned at Eddie, and then went back to talking the woman into buying a lizard.

"I think," Liza said with a smile, "I have an idea."

12

Doomed

Liza pulled a bag of doggie treats from the shelves.

"This is no time to shop," Melody said.

Liza shook her head. "This is ammunition," she said, "for a leprechaun war."

Howie smiled. "I get it. If we plant treats on Mr. McDawgle, then Diamond might lick him."

"That's easy to say," Melody said. "But how in the world are we going to do that?"

Liza snapped her fingers. "We'll just be nice," she told her friends.

"Nice?" Eddie asked. "When does being nice ever help?"

"Just make sure Diamond gets back in the store," Liza told Eddie. "I'll do the rest."

Liza marched toward Mr. McDawgle as Eddie sneaked to the front of the store and opened the door for Diamond. Mr. McDawgle had his back to Liza and was showing an ant farm to a little kid.

Liza tapped Mr. McDawgle on the shoulder. "Excuse me," she said in her most polite voice. "I have something for you."

As soon as he turned around, she reached up and dumped a bag of doggie treats right over Mr. McDawgle's head. Mr. McDawgle sputtered and wiped at the crumbs on his face.

"Go," Eddie said, pushing Diamond toward Mr. McDawgle. Diamond sniffed the air and got a whiff of the treats. That was all he needed. He bounded toward Mr. McDawgle, put his giant paws on the short man's shoulders, and licked his cheek.

"NO!!!!!" Mr. McDawgle screamed. He jumped away from Diamond and scratched the spot where Diamond had kissed him.

"Oops," Liza said with a sly smile. "Sorry about that."

The four kids stared at Mr. McDawgle.

He didn't look any different. Had Diamond's kiss changed him? Howie had to be sure.

"Is it okay if we return those pet supplies we bought and get our money back?" Howie asked.

"But of course," Mr. McDawgle said, rubbing at his cheek until it was red. "I wouldn't want you to keep something you didn't want."

Eddie waited until he got outside the pet shop to cheer. "We did it!"

"We broke the spell of the Blarney stone all right," Howie said.

Melody patted Liza on the back. "You did it!" Melody told her friend. "You and Diamond."

Liza gave Diamond a hug around the neck. "We do have one more problem," Liza reminded her friends. "Mrs. Jeepers. She kissed the Blarney stone, too. She'll be able to talk us into doing anything she wants unless she gets kissed by a beast!"

Melody gulped. "We're doomed!"

13

The Real Beast

"No problem," Eddie said. "We'll just use the rest of the doggie treats."

"There aren't many left," Liza said. "Do you think it will work?"

"Sure," Eddie said, but he didn't get the chance to find out because Diamond jumped up and ate the treats right out of his hand.

"No!" Eddie yelled.

"I hope he doesn't get sick," Melody said.

Eddie sank down in the clover. "It would serve him right if he did get sick. He just ate our hopes to get rid of a superpowerful blarney vampire teacher."

"There's got to be another way," Howie said.

"We'd better think fast because here she comes," Melody said. Sure enough,

Mrs. Jeepers was walking right down the sidewalk toward the kids. She was frowning and one finger reached for the green brooch pinned at her throat.

Eddie tossed his baseball cap onto the ground and dug through his pockets. He held up a four-day-old piece of cookie, covered with lint. "Will this do?" he asked.

"That's disgusting," Liza said.

"It's better than nothing," Melody admitted.

"Hi, Mrs. Jeepers," Eddie said as his teacher walked up. "I have a surprise for you."

Mrs. Jeepers' finger stopped before it touched the green brooch at her neck and she smiled at Eddie. "That is very thoughtful of you," she said.

Eddie pushed the cookie toward Mrs. Jeepers' face. "Thank you," she said. "I will save this for later. She quickly dropped the lint-covered cookie into her purse and dusted off her hands.

"Next week at school, we will have so much fun," Mrs. Jeepers told the students. "We will finish every page in our math book."

The kids nodded and smiled. "That sounds wonderful," Liza said. Then she shook her head. Had she really said that?

Diamond cowered on the ground, staying away from Mrs. Jeepers. Liza sighed and hugged Diamond as their teacher walked toward the pet shop. "I guess Diamond doesn't like cookies."

"Diamond likes anything with sugar," Eddie told her. "He's just like me."

"What did you say?" Liza asked.

Howie held up his hands. "Forget this sugar talk. Forget about candy."

"Forget about having fun, too," Melody said miserably. "Mrs. Jeepers is going to work us to death at school. Since she has the gift of blarney, we won't be able to stop her."

"Wait," Liza said slowly. "Eddie just

gave me a great idea. I think it might work, but I know he won't like it."

Eddie groaned and held his stomach. The whole Blarney stone business was making him sick. "I'd do anything to stop Mrs. Jeepers."

"Anything?" Liza asked. When Eddie nodded, Liza told him her idea.

"You have to do it," Howie said. "It's the only way."

Eddie started to complain. He thought about screaming. He wanted to jump up and down, but he didn't. He knew Liza and Howie were right. It was up to him to save the day.

"Wait!" Eddie yelled to Mrs. Jeepers. She paused with her hand on the door to the pet shop.

Eddie rushed up to his teacher and said, "I have another surprise for you, Mrs. Jeepers." Before he could change his mind, Eddie grabbed Mrs. Jeepers' hand and kissed it with a big, wet, sloppy kiss.

Mrs. Jeepers blushed. "Now *that* was a surprise."

Howie, Melody, and Liza rushed up beside Eddie and Mrs. Jeepers. "Are we still going to have to finish our entire math book next week at school?" Liza asked Mrs. Jeepers.

Mrs. Jeepers stared at her hand and shook her head. "Of course not. That would be too much work." Mrs. Jeepers sighed and said, "I think I will go home now. This has been a very busy weekend."

The four kids watched their teacher walk away. "We did it!" Howie said. "We got rid of Mrs. Jeepers' gift of blarney."

"Eddie did it," Liza said.

"I don't understand," Melody said. "Why did Eddie's kiss work?"

Liza giggled. "It's simple. Eddie is the biggest beast of all!"

St. Patrick's Day Activities

Pet Shop Word Search

The animals in the Clover Patch Pet Store are hiding. Can you find these animal words hidden below? The words are horizontal, vertical, and even backward!

Words: BIRD, TOAD, KITTEN, HAMSTER, CAT, FISH, NEWT, LIZARD

Answers on page 84.

Clover Patch Matchup

Match the name of each Bailey School Kid to the item he or she bought at the Clover Patch Pet Store. Remember, each kid bought two items.

Liza	Muzzle
	Fish Food
Melody	Fuzzy Mouse Toy
	Dog Bowl
Howie	Fish
	Newt
Eddie	Dog Collar
	Kitty Litter

Answers on page 84.

Memory Game

It's time to test your memory. Look at the picture on page 10 for fifteen seconds. Ask a friend or family member to time you. Then read the questions below. See how many questions you can answer without looking back at the picture. No peeking!

1. How many dog bones are in the picture?

2. What is behind Mr. McDawgle: a fish tank, bird cages, or boxes of dog food?

3. How many toy mice are in the display case?

4. Which one of the following items is *not* in the picture: dog leashes, balls, collars, hamster wheels, or a cash register?

5. Is Mr. McDawgle wearing a hat?

Answers on page 84.

Shamrock Shake

Here's a yummy green treat that can't be beat! It's as easy as one, two, three. You may need an adult to help you with this recipe.

You will need:

Mint or pistachio ice cream or frozen yogurt
1/2 cup milk
A blender

1. Put three scoops of ice cream and the milk into a blender.
2. Make sure the lid on the blender is tight. Then blend until smooth.
3. Pour the shake into two glasses and share with a friend!

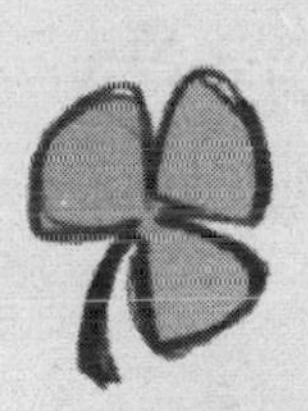

Pot-of-Gold Crossword Puzzle

Now that you have read *Leprechauns Don't Play Fetch*, can you answer the questions in this puzzle?

Across

1. Who buys a muzzle at the pet store?
2. What kind of pet will the kids *not* find at Mr. McDawgle's pet store?
3. What kind of pet does Eddie take care of?
4. What does Eddie's aunt give the kids money to buy?

Down

5. What does Mr. McDawgle sell at his store?
6. What is the name of Aunt Mathilda's pet?

Answers on page 84.

Answer Key

Pet Shop Word Search page 78

Clover Patch Matchup page 79

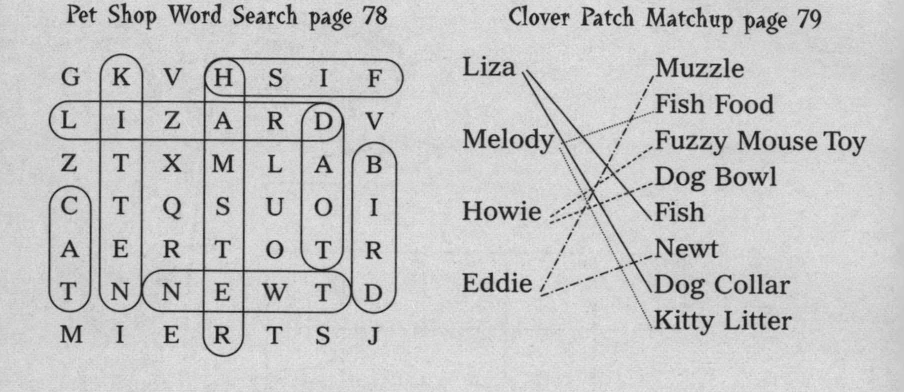

Memory Game page 80

1. Eight
2. A fish tank
3. Three
4. A hamster wheel
5. Yes

Pot-of-Gold Crossword Puzzle page 83

Debbie Dadey and Marcia Thornton Jones have fun writing stories together. When they both worked at an elementary school in Lexington, Kentucky, Debbie was the school librarian and Marcia was a teacher. During their lunch break in the school cafeteria, they came up with the idea of the Bailey School Kids.

Recently Debbie and her family moved to Fort Collins, Colorado. Marcia and her husband still live in Kentucky, where she continues to teach. How do these authors write together? They talk on the phone and use computers and fax machines!

Learn more about Debbie and Marcia at their Web site, www.BaileyKids.com!

❑ BSK 0-439-04398-0	#38	Ninjas Don't Bake Pumpkin Pie	$3.99 US
❑ BSK 0-439-04399-9	#39	Dracula Doesn't Rock and Roll	$3.99 US
❑ BSK 0-439-04401-4	#40	Sea Monsters Don't Ride Motorcycles	$3.99 US
❑ BSK 0-439-04400-6	#41	The Bride of Frankenstein Doesn't Bake Cookies	$3.99 US
❑ BSK 0-439-21582-X	#42	Robots Don't Catch Chicken Pox	$3.99 US
❑ BSK 0-439-21583-8	#43	Vikings Don't Wear Wrestling Belts	$3.99 US
❑ BSK 0-439-21584-6	#44	Ghosts Don't Rope Wild Horses	$3.99 US
❑ BSK 0-439-36803-0	#45	Wizards Don't Wear Graduation Gowns	$3.99 US
❑ BSK 0-439-36805-7	#46	Sea Serpents Don't Juggle Water Balloons	$3.99 US

❑ BSK 0-439-04396-4	Bailey School Kids Super Special #4: Mrs. Jeepers in Outer Space	$3.99 US
❑ BSK 0-439-21585-4	Bailey School Kids Super Special #5: Mrs. Jeepers' Monster Class Trip	$3.99 US
❑ BSK 0-439-30641-8	Bailey School Kids Super Special #6: Mrs. Jeepers On Vampire Island	$3.99 US
❑ BSK 0-439-40831-8	Bailey School Kids Holiday Special: Aliens Don't Carve Jack-o'-lanterns	$3.99 US
❑ BSK 0-439-40832-6	Bailey School Kids Holiday Special: Mrs. Claus Doesn't Climb Telephone Poles	$3.99 US
❑ BSK 0-439-33338-5	Bailey School Kids Thanksgiving Special: Swampmonsters Don't Chase Wild Turkeys	$3.99 US

Available wherever you buy books, or use this order form

Scholastic Inc., P.O. Box 7502, Jefferson City, MO 65102

Please send me the books I have checked above. I am enclosing $______ (please add $2.00 to cover shipping and handling). Send check or money order — no cash or C.O.D.s please.

Name ____________________

Address ____________________

City ____________________ State/Zip ____________________

Please allow four to six weeks for delivery. Offer good in the U.S. only. Sorry, mail orders are not available to residents of Canada. Prices subject to change.

BSK902